W9-BSQ-737

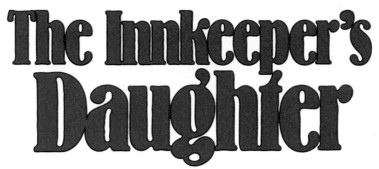

The Innkeeper's Daughter

A Delightful Discovery of a Wonderful Adventure

Written by
JILL BRISCOE

Illustrated by Russ Flint

**Published by Focus on the Family Publishing
Pomona, CA 91799.**

Distributed by Word Books, Dallas, Texas.

Copyright © 1989 by Jill Briscoe
No part of this book may be reproduced or copied
without written permission from the publisher.

Designed by Julie Mammano

Library of Congress Catalog Card Number 89-11851
ISBN 0-929608-18-6

ETURAH'S mother called from the inn's back door: "Keturah, come here quickly."

"Coming," Keturah shouted as she scurried out of the animal yard.

"Where have you been?" her mother demanded, hands on her hips, looking quite cross. "In the stable with the donkeys no doubt."

"I...I," began Keturah.

"Never mind," her mother said, waving impatiently. "The inn is full. Go and get the sign and put it up."

Keturah ran to get the big sign that said, *No Room.* But because her left foot turned outward and her leg was too short, she limped as she ran.

It wasn't often they had to hang the sign on the inn's huge wooden door. Tonight business was better than it had been for a long time.

"Why are so many people coming here?" Keturah asked as she struggled to carry the heavy sign.

"The Romans are doing a census," her mother answered. "They're counting everyone to see how many people live in this country."

"Why does everyone have to come here?"

"They don't," her mother said, laughing. "The Romans made people go to the town where they were born. Only those born in Bethlehem come here."

Keturah gave her mother a puzzled look and said, "Why are they—"

"Keturah!" her mother interrupted, throwing her hands in the air. "I don't have time for anymore questions. I'm busy! Put up the sign so we won't be pestered by anymore people looking for rooms. Then go and play."

"Let me help bake bread. Please. Please!"

"Not now. You would be in the way," her mother said, scurrying away.

Keturah muttered to herself as she hung the sign on the door: "That's what they always say to me. Stay out of the way. You're too little."

BETHLEHEM
INN

NO
ROOM

That evening, Keturah slipped back to her quiet hideout in the stable. She loved to be with the animals, but most of all she loved Elam, her donkey. She felt close to him because he had a deformed leg like hers.

"Hello, Elam," she whispered as she stroked her favorite donkey's fur.

"Hee-haw, hee-haw, hee-haw," the donkey brayed, pawing the ground and nudging the door as if he wanted to go out.

"What's the matter, Elam? You're so restless. Don't be afraid of the noises outside," assured Keturah.

Keturah followed the animal's eyes toward the stable's entrance. Another donkey brayed outside the stable, so she headed to the door and held up the oil lamp to see who was there. "Hello," said a man holding the donkey's reins. He had a kind face and tired brown eyes. "And who are you?" he asked, smiling.

"Keturah," she replied, looking at the ground. "I'm the innkeeper's daughter."

"I'm Joseph," said the man, "and this is my wife, Mary."

When Keturah looked into his face, he seemed to be a calm man just like her father. Keturah held the donkey's bridle while Joseph helped Mary off the animal. She had beautiful, wide eyes and long, black, silky hair. She was going to have a baby! She was very big, indeed. Keturah knew that meant the baby was coming soon.

At that moment, Keturah's mother rushed into the stable, looking flustered. "I'm sorry about this," she said to Joseph, "but the inn is absolutely overflowing. There's no room at all. Our entire family had to give up their beds."

"This will do fine," Joseph assured her.

"Yes, of course," added Mary.

"You...you mean you're go...going to sleep here in the stable?" Keturah said.

"It's a bit dirty, but we clean it out every day," Keturah's mother offered, looking around with doubt. Then she turned to her daughter and said, "Keturah, don't just stand there, get some fresh straw."

"Yes, Mother," she said, limping out of the stable as fast as she could.

Keturah helped spread the straw around the dirt floor.

"I wish you could have my bed," Keturah said softly. Mary smiled and said, "Thank you, but we can stay here. You've made us feel quite at home.

"We're grateful we're not sleeping under the stars tonight," said Joseph. "It's cold and windy out."

"May I sleep in the stall with Elam tonight?" Keturah asked her mother.

"In here? Joseph and Mary need their rest. You might be in the way."

"Keturah is welcome to stay with us," Mary offered.

"Yes, certainly," added Joseph.

"All right then," said her mother, "as long as you're up in time to help with breakfast."

"I will be! I will be!" Keturah said, dancing up and down.

When everyone settled down for the night, Keturah squeezed into a small space in Elam's stall. Tired out by the busy doings of the day, she soon fell asleep.

Keturah awoke sometime during the middle of the night, thinking she was dreaming. She heard a baby cry. Still half asleep, she bumped her head on Elam, startling him as she crawled out of the stall.

''You had the baby!'' she said with surprise when she saw the infant cradled in Mary's arms.

''We named him Jesus,'' Mary said. Her face shone with happiness.

''He's so tiny.'' Keturah gazed with wonder at the baby's puckered mouth, chubby cheeks and head covered with dark hair. She had believed it was the worst thing in the world to be the baby in the family. But looking at Jesus, she thought maybe being the baby wasn't so bad after all!

Joseph's eyes smiled like the stars outside the stable. He was so pleased. Even the animals made happy noises to welcome the baby.

''Hee-haw, hee-haw,'' Elam brayed.

''Bah, bah,'' bleated the sheep.

''They're saying welcome to baby Jesus,'' said Keturah and laughed.

Suddenly, there was a loud commotion outside the stable. The shepherd boys, Aaron, Jacob, Hiram, and Zeb, tumbled into the stable and crowded around Mary and the baby.

"Look! Here's the baby," Zeb exclaimed.

"He's in the manger, just like the angel said," Aaron shouted.

"Angel! What do you mean?" cried Keturah, tugging at his robe.

"We were watching the sheep," said Aaron, gesturing excitedly.

"The angel told us not to be afraid," said Hiram.

"I wasn't afraid," added Aaron proudly.

"Yes, you were," said Zeb. "All of us were. The angel was so big and bright."

"What else did the angel say?" asked Keturah.

" 'I bring you good news of a great joy which will come to all the people; for to you is born this day in the city of David a Savior.' "

"Can you believe it?" Hiram said, his voice filled with awe. "This baby is Christ the Lord!"

"Do you know what else happened?" Zeb didn't wait for an answer. "A bright light from heaven lit up the whole sky."

"Lots more angels came!" Aaron said. "They were all over the sky and the fields."

"Thousands of them," shouted Zeb. "They sang a beautiful song."

"What did they sing?" Mary asked.

Hiram answered, "They sang, 'Glory to God in the highest, and on earth peace, good will toward men.'"

"Then the angels just disappeared," Jacob exclaimed. "So we ran all the way here to see the baby."

"Come on," Zeb said. "Let's go tell everyone in town about the baby Jesus."

"Yes," Hiram put in, "we'll let them know the Savior is here."

Mary smiled at baby Jesus as the shepherds hurried away.

When Mary and baby Jesus fell asleep, Keturah tiptoed back into the stall. "What does this mean 'Jesus is the Savior?'" she whispered to Elam. "The baby is so tiny, so helpless, but angels sang Him a birthday song and shepherds came to worship Him."

The donkey nudged her hand with his soft, warm nose as if to say, "I know this baby, Keturah. How glad I am He is in my stable."

It had been the most wonderful night of her life, Keturah decided. Maybe being little wasn't so bad after all.

In the morning, Keturah brought Joseph and Mary slices of warm bread her mother had baked. She told her mother and father and some of the servants about baby Jesus, and they came to see Him in the stable.

Later that day, Keturah helped Joseph lead the donkeys out to pasture. Joseph's donkey was so old, she wondered how it had made it all the way to Bethlehem.

"Poor donkey," Keturah said quietly.

"Yes," said Joseph. "This donkey's time for service is about over."

"I hope you won't go anywhere else," blurted Keturah.

"Don't worry about us. We're staying here in Bethlehem," Joseph replied.

"I wish there was room in the inn," Keturah said. "I want to help Mary with the baby."

"Well, now," Joseph said kindly, "you can still help us even though we won't be staying at the inn. I'm looking for a place to live nearby, and Mary will be glad for another pair of hands. I'll see if I can work for the village carpenter."

The next day, Joseph and Mary found a small room in a house near the inn. Keturah helped to get them settled.

"My father said your donkey can stay with us," she told them. "Elam will be happy to have the company."

"How kind of your father," said Mary softly.

When the time came for Joseph and Mary to dedicate baby Jesus, they invited Keturah to go with them to the temple at Jerusalem.

''It's our custom to give an offering to God for the baby's safe arrival,'' Joseph explained.

Keturah turned to her father and said, ''Please, may I go with them?''

''Yes, you may go,'' her father replied. ''There's not as much work now that the visitors are returning to their own cities.''

So Keturah, Joseph, Mary, and the baby journeyed to Jerusalem to dedicate Jesus in the temple. But they had to stop often because Joseph's old donkey couldn't travel as fast as Elam.

When they arrived at the temple it was late, so Keturah said, "I'll tie the donkeys." She secured the animals to a post and then ran to catch up with Mary and Joseph.

Keturah arrived just in time to see Simeon, a very old man, take Jesus in his arms and praise God. "Lord, now I can leave here in peace," he said. "I have seen the Savior you have given to the world. He is the Light that will shine for all the nations."

At that same moment, Anna, an even older lady, came by and exclaimed, ''Thank you God for this special child. The Savior has finally come.''

Then Anna started calling to everyone milling around inside the temple to come and see Jesus. Keturah smiled proudly. *Why, Jesus is famous already,* she thought to herself.

Busy happy months passed quickly. Keturah looked after the new donkey as well as her own beloved Elam. She saw Joseph and Mary every day.

One afternoon Mary asked Keturah to hold the baby while she spoke to a man who had come to the door selling baskets.

"Baby Jesus, you're so light," whispered Keturah.

She felt so happy, she thought she would burst. She was such a little girl, but Mary said she was big enough to cradle Jesus in her arms. Keturah didn't know how long she held the Christ. How do you count the moments when God is in your arms?

She crooned a cradle song to Jesus. When He acted like He was hungry, she said soothingly, "There, there, Little One. Your mother is coming; your mother is coming."

The next day on her way to Mary and Joseph's house, she met the shepherd boys coming down the road talking excitedly.

"Did you see their camels?" Aaron exclaimed.

"Yes, and what about their clothes?" Jacob replied breathlessly.

"They were carrying expensive boxes," interrupted Aaron.

"They must have come from far away," said Zeb. "Their food bags were empty, and they looked worn out from the journey."

"They were wise men from the East," chipped in Hiram.

"Who are you talking about?" Keturah asked. "And where did these men go?"

"To the house where Mary, Joseph, and baby Jesus live," said Aaron.

Keturah ran, limping down the street with the shepherds racing ahead of her. When they arrived at the house, the wise men in their kingly clothes were kneeling around Mary and the baby. The men were giving Jesus expensive gifts.

''We saw His star in the east and came to worship Him,'' one of them said to Mary and Joseph.

Keturah and the shepherds stood in the doorway, watching in awe. Her father had also heard the commotion and followed them into the room.

When the men started to leave,
Keturah's father came forward and said,
"We have rooms in our inn, if you would
like to stay here tonight."

They thanked him kindly, said good-bye
to Mary and Joseph, went to water their
camels and settled down for a good sleep.

But this was not a night to sleep, and there certainly was no sleep for King Herod. His Majesty was mad! The three wise men had stopped at the palace in Jerusalem expecting to find Jesus there.

"Where is the new baby, the King of the Jewish people?" they asked. "We saw His star in far-off eastern lands and have come to worship Him."

When King Herod heard this he was upset. He didn't know where the baby was, but he pretended he was pleased about the news of His birth.

"Go and look for Him," Herod said to the wise men. "Then come tell me where He is so I can worship Him, too." He really didn't want to honor Jesus at all, but planned to kill the baby. He was jealous and didn't want any other king in the country but himself.

But the wise men didn't go back to Herod. Instead, at the inn, they fell into a deep sleep. In the middle of the night, they awoke suddenly because they all had a strange dream. God warned them not to go see Herod. He told them to take a different road back to their country. So they got up and called for Keturah's father. "Prepare our camels. We must leave right away."

Keturah's father woke his wife and daughter. She wondered what all the fuss was about when he sent her to the stable to prepare the animals for the journey. The huge camels weren't nearly as easy to manage as the donkeys.

After the wise men left, Keturah went back to the stable to check on Elam. Then Joseph and Mary appeared in the doorway with baby Jesus. ''Keturah, saddle the donkey,'' Joseph said urgently. ''We must leave at once.''

''But-but it's late at night,'' Keturah stammered.

''An angel came,'' said Joseph. ''King Herod is searching for our son. He plans to kill Jesus. We must hurry to Egypt and hide.''

''Kill Jesus?'' she gasped. ''Oh, Joseph, no! I don't want you to go,'' sobbed Keturah. ''I love you. I love baby Jesus.''

''We know,'' said Mary gently.

As she watched Joseph quickly bridle the donkey, Elam brayed, ''Hee-haw. Hee-haw.'' He pawed the ground as if he wanted to go, too. Keturah kissed the animal's silky face and tried to quiet him, but he brayed all the louder.

Keturah thought about how much faster they could go if Mary and baby Jesus had Elam to ride instead of their old donkey. Suddenly she felt that she should give them Elam. But how could she ever give him up? She had loved Elam since he was born.

Then Keturah thought of baby Jesus and recalled King Herod's threats. She turned to her father and said, "May I give baby Jesus my donkey?"

"Elam, your pet? Are you sure?"

"Yes, Father. Joseph's donkey is so slow. Please, let them have Elam so they can go faster."

"All right, he's yours to give."

Keturah handed Elam's reins to Joseph, watching as he helped Mary onto the donkey's back.

"Thank you, Keturah," Joseph said.

"We will always remember you," added Mary.

Keturah stood on her tiptoes and kissed baby Jesus good-bye.

Elam rubbed his soft nose in Keturah's hair and nudged her shoulder as if to say good-bye. She scratched his ear, and he brayed with glee.

Then she stood in the doorway, watching as Joseph, Mary, precious baby Jesus, and Elam disappeared down the road. It was hard to see them go, and her eyes filled with tears. Despite her sadness, Keturah felt warm and happy inside, knowing she had given Jesus her very best gift.